Jinx and Draco in the Fairy Realms-

Book 1

MERKLE

AND THE

HEDGE FAIRIES

Written by
Katie Martinez

Illustrated by
Carlos A. Saavedra

Jinx & Draco in the Fairy Realms

www.JinxAndDraco.com

To request permission, contact the author at

Katie@JinxAndDraco.com

Edited by Deborah DeNicola
Illustrated by Carlos A. Saavedra
Published by Katie Martinez

CONTENTS

<u>Introduction</u>

The story of Jinx and Draco and the Fairy Realms is based on our sweet pets. Jinx escapes, ever so often, to the backyard when Draco wants to go outside. Sometimes she disappears for several hours and I always imagine where she goes on her adventures because she always comes back home in just a little while. Jinx and Draco always know just exactly what to do to make fun happen on lazy afternoons.

These tales are based on my ideas of the adventures that a little black kitty cat can get herself into while always making it back before bedtime. I do hope you enjoy this magical tale of the adventures that Draco, our large, but sweet, Black Labrador/German Shepard mix, is also excited to participate in with Jinx.

Some of the mystical elements of the book include crystal energies. Rosy Q is a hobgoblin who uses crystals as light magic to help heal or guide Jinx and Draco on their adventures.

Jinx and Draco see the importance of planting more green spaces for their new fairy friends to have more land to live. They want more people to be aware of the importance of green spaces in our towns and cities across America. In the end we all have to share this wonderful world with the animals and other creatures who may be hiding in plain sight. Who knows, maybe you have fairies living in the hedges behind your house. I know we do.

With much love and light,

Katie, Jinx, and Draco

Chapter One
Just a Typical Tuesday

*J*inx sat on the windowsill and drifted in and out of a cat nap on a typical Tuesday afternoon. Finally, Draco stopped barking at the mailman and trotted over to take a nap. All was quiet in the house except for the tick-tock of the clock. He lay down on the couch next to her. Jinx's long black tail swished back and forth, back and forth, back and forth, in perfect time with the clock. The motion of the clock and tail together put Draco into a trance that hypnotized both him and Jinx into a hazy daydream.

As she lay next to the large picture window, the sun glistened down on her soft radiant black fur. She was a beautiful cat and she knew it as she admired her reflection in the window. While she gazed out the window, she stared at The Magnolia Tree. The Spanish moss blew softly in the gentle breeze. She looked around the backyard, becoming mesmerized by the yellow orchids that blossomed in the flower house. Even though her life seemed boring, she suddenly found some pleasure in her typical Tuesday. Jinx realized she was pleasantly comfortable in her homestead.

Everyone including Jinx and Draco loved having a big backyard mostly because they loved to plant flowers and herbs. Jinx loved all the places as far as her eyes could see, but her favorite place to visit was the hedges. She seemed right at home in the hedges and always felt free as she sat on the fence post looking over the top of them. She always wondered and imagined what adventure she could go on past those bushes. Everyone loved sitting in the backyard admiring the flowers, the birds, and especially the butterflies.

Suddenly she woke up out of her daydream, and her collar jingled as she shifted her body. She intentionally took a closer look for any ounce of excitement. Something or someone out there needed to save her and Draco in their hypnotized state.

All of a sudden while looking out of the window, she saw a poof of golden dust fly into the air. Her fur stood on end and her ears perked up so she could hear what was going on. Just then, she saw a strange, mystifying creature that walked with sheer determination towards the back door. He looked angry and concerned but mostly offended as gold dust seemed to float all around him as he flailed his arms. She walked over to the back door and saw him through the window.

He was only about as tall as she was but was shaped like her human friends. The curious creature had a large bumpy nose and it was snarled in disgust with the obvious experiment that had gone wrong. His brown robe was caked in gold dust and his prayer staff glistened with the mess up.

All Jinx could do was laugh at the silly creature; it was hard to take him seriously with golden dust flying everywhere.

She tried to stay quiet, the last thing she wanted to do was to get Draco stirred back up and barking again. She heard the silly overprotective pooch making a gruff noise, snorting and starting to move.

"Oh, no," she thought, and before she could stop him, he turned the corner and barked loudly.

"Danger, danger! Jinx, back up he is a stranger and could hurt us just like the mailman!!"

Jinx rolled her crisp green eyes and looked back into the eyes of the loud and crazed mutt. Sarcastically she said, "*Stranger danger, stranger danger,* you never let me have any fun."

Just then, the human must have heard Draco's hubbub and came over to open the door for Draco to go outside.

This was her chance.

She had a chance to escape and see what this mystical creature was all about.

Draco clumsily jumped at the door and the creature ran out of sight. Jinx knew that Draco would sniff him out and possibly injure the curious old fella so she had to be part of the distraction so she could get outside too.

Draco was out of control as he jumped and barked while the human frantically tried to open up the door.

In all of the commotion, Jinx slipped next to Draco's black fur and blended in and as soon as the door was open, out she flew while Draco bumbled after her. She felt free as she ran toward the hedges, where the curious visitor had fled to hide behind the flower house.

Once the oversized mutt had forgotten his mission to protect her from the stranger, she followed the trail of gold dust back behind

the flower house to the hedges where she
found the grumpy creature on the ground as
he trembled in terror.

"Hi, I'm Jinx," she said as she looked into
his spirited hazel eyes.

His eyes softened and he smiled at her.
"I know," he said.

Jinx was shocked as she didn't realize
that he knew her. She felt honored but
curious. "How do you know me?" she
questioned.

"I was with you when you were born,"
said the creature. "I'm Merkle, the hobgoblin
from the Hedge Fairy Realm."

Jinx was shocked but intrigued by her

new friend.

"I am the mystical advisor to all of the hedge fairies, and I also guide animals who are lost to find someone to take care of them." He continued, "I found you in the hedges just down the way and guided your human friend to find you."

"That's truly amazing and thank you for that." Jinx turned her head to one side and asked, "but why did you have gold dust everywhere?"

After a brief pause, Merkle turned to Jinx and said, "to get your attention." Looking into her eyes Merkle explained, "We need you to bring balance to the humans and hedge fairies. The goddess Freda wants to have a special animal come and carry messages to and from the humans and she chose you."

Jinx was astonished. "Me?" she questioned, "Why me?"

Merkle sighed and said, "You have a great sense of curiosity and black cats are precious to the hedge fairies and ... your human family loves to plant flowers and hedges which is what we need more of," he paused before continuing.

He looked down at the ground and traced lines with his pointed-toed shoes "Well, there is this girl hobgoblin named Rosy Q, and like me, she loves mysterious black cats and I know that you can do a good job . . . and we need you . . . they need you . . . we all need you to do this important . . ."

Before he could finish Draco had traced Merkle's scent and ran back over to bark and lunge toward them. Jinx tried to get him to stop but when she turned back to talk to Merkle he had already high-tailed it back into the hedges.

Suddenly, the hedges started to spin, and an opening appeared that looked like an entrance into a dark portal.

Merkle turned and she heard him exclaim, "Freda will be back tomorrow night on the start of the full moon at midnight for your answer."

Before she could say anything else, he was gone with a flash.

Jinx was concerned about what her task would be. She was full of questions. How would she know how to complete it? How could she even give Merkle an answer if she didn't even know what she was to do? And who in the world is Freda? But those answers would have to wait until the full moon.

All of a sudden, the human reached down and picked her up and as Draco trotted along beside them, and they made their way back into the house. She soon found herself back on the windowsill in the house on a typical Tuesday afternoon, except now it was anything but typical. Her tail was swishing back and forth, back and forth, back and forth, in perfect time with the clock. Hypnotized again, Draco calmed down beside her. Now she found herself curious with excitement. She had to say yes, if only just to help with typical Tuesdays.

"What did he want? Who was that? Is he trying to hurt you? Does he want you to go away with him?" Draco hysterically questioned Jinx.

Finally, the humans had gone to sleep for the night and Draco could ask these ever so important questions.

Jinx looked into Draco's big brown eyes saying, "Draco, I will never leave you and the humans, but I need a sense of purpose for my life."

After a long silence, Draco said, "then I want you to go help the hedge fairies."

Although Draco seemed a little sad, Jinx knew he always had her best interest in mind.

Jinx gazed into the misty darkness of the backyard. She realized that the nighttime brought out much different sights and sounds. The bright yellow orchids seemed to dull in the shadows. The hedges cast dark deep shaded areas.

She listened to hear the frogs and crickets sing the night songs and her mind drifted back to her first night in the house. One of the humans found her in the hedges, scared and lonely, as she cried out for help that night. She was truly grateful for her life in the house and would never give up that world, even if she needed more purpose in her life.

As she looked over to Draco and remembered back when Draco was so excited to see her and meet with her for the first time. He was so big and bouncy and LOUD, but his heart, she knew was golden, and she has always loved him like the father that she never had. Her heart was full. Plus, they could always get into some fun trouble together.

As she drifted off to sleep, she dreamed of her newfound mission. She dreamed of magical powers and enchantments. Her missions were filled with excitement and importance.

After an hour had passed, she was awakened by a light that pierced through the picture window. She slowly woke up and cleared her sleepy eyes to see a ravishing lavender figure. Jinx stood up and stretched long and tall on the windowsill and heard a beautiful voice speak as she still tried to focus her eyes.

"Hello, Jinx . . . I'm Freda, the Goddess of the Hedge Fairies. Merkle expressed many wonderful stories about your bravery. We would love for you to come and help us better understand humans. Our fairy realms suffer due to fewer hedges, flowers, trees, and herb gardens. Instead of fighting the changes in our world, the fairy realm leaders have decided

that we would like to join forces with the
humans."

Jinx whispered to herself, "I must still
be dreaming, this can't be happening for real.
Right in my very own backyard?"

The goddess came closer to the window
and continued, "Please help us out. At twilight

meet us by The Magnolia Tree beside the flower house tomorrow night. But for now, you need your rest. Not a single whisper of this to the humans for now, sweet Jinx. A plan will be discussed upon your arrival in the hedge fairy realm." Freda then vanished into a silvery mist.

As Jinx turned back to lie down, Draco was standing behind her with his eyes wide and his jaw dropped.

Jinx said, "Draco if you say a word of this to the humans, I will never be able to trust you again."

"My lips are sealed my dear Jinx, you have become a very important figure with an important mission," Draco said with admiration.

Just as Jinx still tried to distinguish between reality and her dreams, she drifted off to sleep again.

The next morning was filled with excitement, the humans prepared for a big day as they hustled and bustled with lots of jittery behavior. Jinx heard laughter throughout the house and she felt she would burst with anticipation.

After her human family gave her morning backrubs and breakfast, she decided to meditate on the choices to be made later that afternoon. She sat up on the windowsill and looked at all the butterflies and birds that skittered about in the backyard.

Her thoughts drifted to wondering what Merkle was doing. What would the hedge fairies look like? Would they like her? So many unanswered questions in her riddle of a predicament. Although the goddess did give her more insight as to what role she would play in this fantasy realm, she was still nervous. The butterflies in the backyard seemed to have entered her stomach as she thought about her new responsibility.

Meanwhile, at the Hedge Fairy Village, Merkle and the fairies were energetic as they started the preparations for the full moon and initiation ceremony.

"Hurry with that collar, Rocky, make sure to polish that crystal, did we make sure that purple was the correct color?" Merkle nervously questioned Rocky, the jeweler.

All of a sudden, the head fairy, Merlina, came buzzing up to Merkle. "What about Draco?" Merlina calmly asked. "Draco is a big part of Jinx's life; he is like a father to her."

"Hmmmm," said Merkle, "That crazy mutt nearly bit my head off the other day, but you're right sweet Merlina, he was just trying to protect her. I guess we do look like curious creatures. How much time do you need to make him a collar too?"

She tilted her head to one side and said, "Well I have my best jeweler coming up with some drawings and designs for him, of course without your permission I haven't continued the process but I'm sure a couple of hours would be enough time."

She looked over to Rocky and gave him a wink and when Merkle turned away she blew him a kiss. Rocky blushed as Merkle turned back around and smiled as he sensed the romance that floated between them in the air.

Merkle said, "Let me meditate on this

and get back to you, we must, of course, ask for permission from Freda before we include the mutt in any way."

"Well, please let me know, I want to make sure they get the very best! Oooooo, I am so excited I could nearly burst with pixie dust," squealed Merlina.

As she sensed everyone was curious as to why she broke her usual calm, cool, and collected demeanor, she straightened her dress, cleared her throat, and said "Back to work." She clapped two times. Rocky blushed as she kissed him on the cheek and fluttered away.

Merkle made his way back under the wise Magnolia Tree. The Magnolia Tree was the hedge fairies sacred spot and the sun always made the prettiest shadows underneath it during mid-day.

Merkle was reminded by the heat of the day that soon it would be summer. Even more special, this full moon just happened to coincide with the fairy holiday, Litha, which the humans called the summer solstice. This holiday was a special time in the hedge fairy's year as it celebrated the end of spring as the official summer holiday began. Traditionally, the hedge fairies plant flower seeds and pumpkins to get ready to make one of their favorite fall-time treats, pumpkin honey marmalade, which they stored for the winter. Since the full moon was the same day as the longest day of the year, Litha would be even more special this year.

The huge tree was blooming big white blossoms which made it glow with a golden sheen. The sun poured down through the branches giving warmth to the grass below. Merkle sat on the ground with his legs crossed and his hands balanced on his knees breathing in the afternoon breeze.

He entered his trance-like state while he chanted, "Cha um ray ommmmmm, Cha um ray ommmmmm."

These meditations were important to clear his mind and calm his personal excitement for the ceremony that was to be held later tonight. He chanted a few minutes longer to focus on inward calm, and cleared his mind ready to communicate with Freda.

"Freda," asked Merkle. "The hedge fairies would like to include Jinx's companion, her father figure, Draco. I know that it is not typical to include animals outside of cats, and especially dogs, into these delicate matters, but he is very important to her. Give me a sign of what we should do?"

All of a sudden, the ground started to tremble, and a streak of red light shot up out of the ground. A second streak of purple emerged beside it. Merkle shielded his eyes and when the quake stopped, he saw a single red ruby crystal, and next to it was a purple amethyst.

Then Freda's voice proclaimed, "Draco must have a collar of gold with a ruby charm for he is regal and king-like. Ruby is the stone of love and this stone will give Draco power to clear blocked emotions and ground himself to think clearly. He will be devoted to protecting Jinx and the other fairies while he keeps a compassionate spirit." She handed the ruby to

Merkle.

"Jinx must have the precious amethyst to guide her on her journeys. The amethyst will help to lead Jinx and provide safe travels by providing creative solutions, insight, and intuition. She will connect to me through the power of the amethyst when she needs guidance." She handed the amethyst to Merkle.

"Together Jinx and Draco can bring communion between the fairy and human world. Let it be so."

With that news, Merkle jumped up and exclaimed, "Thank you, Freda, I know Jinx and Merlina will both love this idea."

Then he recollected that Jinx and Merlina hadn't even met yet. The two ladies seem so much alike that he never even thought about how he had to introduce them later today.

"Nevertheless," he whispered to himself "I am sure they will hit it off just fine. It's Kallan I'm worried about the most." Kallan, another hedge fairy, was Merlina's stepbrother.

He had never been able to get over the fact that he was not king. Merlina had taken the throne from Kallan. Because of his anger he turned to dark magic and shape-shifting spells to cause problems within the Hedge Fairy realm.

"I will have to worry about him later," grumbled Merkle.

With that thought, he turned with a skip holding the crystals in his hand and rushed back to Merlina with the exciting news. Draco would be the first dog ever invited into the hedge fairy realm. Eagerness filled the air with what was shaping up to be a joyful night.

Merlina was beside herself, with the excitement that Draco would also go to the initiation into the hedge fairies. From time to time, she watched Draco from a distance. He always protected his human friends and Jinx. Draco's protection was necessary as the Hedge Fairies and the Flower Fairies sometimes had disagreements. Draco, as added protection, would be welcomed news to the Hedge Fairies.

"Hear ye, hear ye, all hedge fairies
gather in for a meeting," Merlina called out.

All the Hedge Fairies gathered around
the Magnolia Tree to hear the news from their
Queen.

Merlina stood on the podium under the
Magnolia Tree and announced, "Tonight is
to be a night that will live forever in all of our

hearts. We are prepared to welcome our sweet Jinx into the hedge fairy realm along with her trusted guide Draco."

The hedge fairies gasped. Whispers and murmurs were heard, "We've never had a dog as our protector before." "What if he tries to hurt us?"

"Or worse." A gruff, annoyed voice came from the back of the crowd. "As head of security in this realm, I strongly advise leaving the mutt out of this, Merlina. He will do nothing but 'Jinx' us all."

Kallan was a jealous stepbrother to Merlina. He was jealous because he didn't get to rule the land after their father transitioned into the heavenly realm.

"Kallan, you always know just the moment to make an appearance," said Merlina. "Usually the wrong one" she mumbled under her breath. "Your concerns have been noted, now please everyone, let's get to work before we run out of time."

All the fairies hurried and scurried to make the final preparations for the full moon ceremony.

"Kallan," shouted after Merlina, "Wait up." As she fluttered to catch up, she braced herself for his mood.

"What harm will Draco do to us? Freda has given her blessing and she will protect us."

"Merlina, what no one is thinking of is the fact that we have never had a dog even visit our realm. Passing through that portal is one thing for a cat because we all know that cats easily transition to our world, but Draco? What could he possibly transition into?" questioned Kallan sarcastically. "I just hope you're not making a mistake playing with magic. Remember there is always a price to pay when working with unknowns in magical techniques. I would know."

Before Merlina could respond, Kallan transformed into a white cat and turned to leave. "What will I ever do with him?" thought Merlina as Kallan continued to grumble and growl as he walked away.

Merlina made her way back to the scene of preparations. All around The Magnolia

Tree, the fairies fluttered to hang the flower garlands gifted to them by the flower fairies for this special occasion. This gift of flowers was a sign of strengthening between the two realms. Hopefully, this merger with the humans would help them as well.

The colorful flowers of Purple and Red glistened in the afternoon sunshine. Magic was in the air and Merlina took a big deep breath inward and closed her eyes as she imagined the magical night to come.

As she made her way into the cottage, she saw the two Kitchen fairies, Gertie and Mertle, covered in dandelion flour as they baked such lovely honey cakes. On the other end of the kitchen was Geryl. Merlina giggled as she saw him hic-cup as he sampled the sarsaparilla.

Gertie yelled, "Geryl, try not to take too much of that sarsaparilla in before the event we have a big crowd to serve tonight."

Geryl jumped with a startle as the sarsaparilla maker popped and bubbled.

Merlina snuck a sample and kissed

Geryl on the cheek as she fluttered back to the meditation room to find Rosy Q.

In the mediation room, she found Rosy as she packed up her knapsack. Rosy Q was another hobgoblin who followed Merkle into the Hedge realm. Rosy had big crystal aquamarine eyes and wore long beads of Rose Quartz. She must have used some kind of crystal magic spell to enrapture Merkle's heart. Merkle was head over heels in love with Rosy, but he was too afraid to let her know. Although Merlina suspected she knew all along, and the feeling was mutual.

"I will need my book of crystals, my wand, and some crystal dust to guide us through the portal," whispered Rosy.

She turned with a startle, "Oh Merlina dear, I didn't see you standing there. Come in, come in and let me offer you some chamomile tea, my dear."

Merlina said, "Oh Rosy, you don't know how much I want to but there is so much to do. The preparations, the banquet table, and oh my goodness I almost forgot the special treats for our guests, warm milk for Jinx and kibbles for Draco. I do have a question for you, sweet Rosy."

"Well, go ahead, I can listen and pack," said, Rosy.

Merlina continued, "Kallan has concerns and I feel I must address them with you. You have the most experience with magical travel to and from the human realm. Do we have any precautions to take with Draco? When he crosses over will he transition easily as himself? Or something else?"

"There's no way to tell really, but one thing I know is that personality and intentions of the soul do not change when crossing over. Draco is a kind and protective soul so I can't see him causing us harm. I have no concerns," said Rosy.

"Well, fabulous then," Merlina smiled, clasping her hands together. "I will meet you by the portal pathway at the dusking hour Rosy."

With a quick hug, Merlina buzzed out to

finalize the preparations.

Back at the house, with Jinx and Draco, Merkle went to get the answer from Jinx and tell her the good news that Draco was to be included and initiated too. He tapped on the window and of course, Draco couldn't contain his energy. He bounced and yelped as he stumbled over the chair towards the door.

Jinx came over and saw Merkle. "Oh, you're here and I have my answer", Jinx whispered through the glass.

Jinx had to find a way out of the house, so she asked Draco to get the human to open the door for him.

He barked and cried, "Hurry I need out, out, out!!!"

The human came over and opened the door that allowed Jinx to narrowly escape as well. While in the back yard, they make their way over to the flower house.

Behind the flower house and under the lilac tree they met Merkle.

"Before you give your answer Jinx, the

fairies and the goddess Freda have requested to honor Draco as well. He will be your protector and companion as you journey through the portal to the hedge fairy realm."

Draco looked stunned. He turned to Jinx, bowed to her and said, "of course, my lady, it would be an honor to be your protector."

Merkle continued, "Draco we have some concerns as we have never had a dog come into our fairy world. Many are fearful of what will happen, but we know your heart is pure with good intentions. Rosy Q is my sweet friend who will meet you at the halfway point, under the Wise Oak Tree tonight. She will have a book of crystal protections as she has created protective talismans for you, as needed for journeys such as this one."

"Will this be dangerous?" questioned Jinx and Draco at the same time.

Merkle thought a second and said, "It can be. In between your hedge and ours is considered a free land zone, so no one guards this place. That being said, however, I don't foresee any problems along your journey."

"Well, that's good to hear," chuckled Draco.

"For now, here are two stones that you should keep with you. Put them around your neck until she meets you under the Wise Oak at the dusking hour. This is the healing talisman we call the healing quartz and the stunning talisman— the obsidian. Quartz crystal is one of the most powerful crystals of all and will heal you from any injury you may encounter, and it naturally makes any intention stronger. Obsidian is a dark black protection stone and will stun any enemy that you may face."

He hesitated then continued, "The powers of these talismans can only be used three times before needing to be recharged. Please keep these talismans close to you as they should be considered as protectors."

Merkle looked at Jinx and asked one more time, "Will you accept this important task?"

"Yes," Jinx proudly stated, "Yes, I will."

Jinx was delighted with excitement and eager to accept what she was called to do. Now more than ever she felt honored to be chosen for initiation into the hedge fairy realm. Best of all, her dear friend Draco was able to come too.

"Draco," Merkle asked, "will you accept your position as a protector?"

"Yes," Draco said with a tear in his eye, "I am so very honored to accept this position as a protector."

"Thank you, this is great, and I'll see you soon," said Merkle. "Don't forget to be here at this portal right at the dusking hour. It only opens when the sun goes down or when the sun comes up at dawn unless you have the gold dust to open the portal."

With that, the hedge portal spun open with gold dust flying and he was gone in a flash.

CHAPTER 4

KALLAN CAUSES CHAOS

"You mean we're going to have to go through that?" Draco said as he shivered.

"Oh, come on Draco, you didn't think this world was just over this fence, did you?" asked Jinx.

Draco looked worried so Jinx assured him that he would be fine. "Draco, I have been to visit the hedge fairies several times, and rest assured you will make it back here in one piece.

Now, we have to get ready. I have to find a place to hide, for now, it's too risky for me going back in the house. I might not make it back outside later. Go inside and create a distraction for me and remember to be out here at the dusking hour exactly."

Draco galloped off as Jinx called to him, "Here, don't forget the healing quartz. I'll take the obsidian.

After Draco left, Jinx wondered how he was going to fit through the portal. It was a detail that she wasn't sure anyone had thought about. In any event, she said to herself, "I'm sure Merkle and Rosy Q knew exactly what to do, hopefully."

As Merkle made it back into the hedge fairy village he could see purple and red pixie dust as it exploded inside the ceremonial Sacrosanct.

"Do you have any idea what disrespect you are showing to the goddess with this childishness? The Sacrosanct is our sacred space and here you are acting like children,"

Merkle shouted.

The two fairies looked around in shame and embarrassment as they realized that purple and red were glittering all around the sacred place. The Sacrosanct was supposed to be a place of peace but it was nothing but a mess and even the flower gifts were sparkling with this mishap.

"Oh dear, Merkle, we are so sorry for our foolish behavior, I don't know what got into us," the twin fairies cried as they apologized again while they flittered away to get the supplies to clean up the disaster.

Merkle quietly pondered why the twin fairies who normally never fought acted this way. As he observed the scene, he noticed other heated conversations around The Magnolia Tree.

From behind him, he heard sniffles, then Merlina said, "I don't know what has gotten into everyone this afternoon. Since you left, the kitchen has been a disaster with Gertie and Mertle at each other's throats. They even threw honey dough at each other. Geryl sampled and sampled the sarsaparilla which caused even more arguments with those three. There is fighting all around."

All of a sudden Merlina saw a white flash out of the corner of her eye. "Of course," Merlina whispered. "It has to be Kallan putting a spell on everyone. KALLAN!!!"

"Why yes, my dear sister whatever seems to be the trouble?" Kallan questioned as he stepped from behind the tree.

"You have cursed these fairies into not following their true nature" scolded Merlina. "I'm so disappointed in you," she continued.

"You know we are required to follow the wishes of the goddess and here you are causing trouble. Do you want to get us all punished? Undo all of this now, this very instant!!!"

"Blah, blah, blah, Merlina you have no idea what you're getting us all into right now," scowled Kallan.

Merlina could feel such resentment on his breath and she trembled and turned away from him.

Merkle usually tried to stay out of hedge fairy squabbles but he felt somewhat responsible for this anger.

"Come on, Kallan," Merkle gently intervened and pulled him aside. "Kallan, my dear fairy, you have to see the light through the darkness in your heart. Darkness does nothing for a soul but blackens it beyond recognition. Please, my friend, undo this madness and, let's find a place for you to belong in the inner workings of this new merger."

Kallan's eyes lit up with fire with the realization that finally his power would be recognized and with a snap of his finger everyone apologized as the place came to order.

Merkle had the feeling that he wasn't done with Kallan. He could be tricky, so he needed something stronger to keep Kallan at bay, but that would have to wait for now. It was getting closer to the dusking hour.

Merlina dressed in her ceremonial attire and stared into the mirror at her reflection.

Rosy Q came into the room and gawked, "Oh dear, don't you look lovely." Rosy was mesmerized at Merlina's appearance and straightened her crown while they both looked in the mirror.

"I wish father was here for this day, he always dreamed of mixing the fairy and human realm. He would be so proud of us," Merlina hung her head with a tear forming in the corner of her eye.

"He loved you so much Merlina, you have his heart and your mother's beauty. You are the perfect combination of your parents."

Rosy Q had been with Merlina since the hobgoblin realm was destroyed by the ogres. Rosy Q, Merkle and a few other hobgoblins had become a part of the hedge fairy realm. Rosy and Merkle acted as the wise spiritual leaders to her and the other hedge fairies. Hobgoblins were not supposed to fall in love but Merlina thought that the two of them had.

"Oh dear, look at the time, I must be

going to get ready for my travels," exclaimed Rosy. "Meet me in 15 minutes by the hedge portal, the dusking hour is upon us." She rushed off and nearly ran into Kallan who lingered outside of Merlina's bedroom with flowers.

Kallan walked into the room, his face was scowled and hurt. "I try to be nice, but no one sees the good in me. Everyone always gushes over you, '*Merlina has the heart of her father, and the beauty of her mother.*' I will never be as respected as you. Here I was bringing you flowers to wish you luck tonight, but my jealousy has overtaken me once again."

"Oh Kallan," said Merlina, "You have to try to let the light inside you. I am not your enemy; I want to give you a more important job but there is too much darkness in your heart right now."

She hurriedly went out the door as Kallan stared at himself in the full-length mirror. An evil grin came across his face as he got the most outrageously horrific idea. "Merlina will not see this one coming," he laughed as his eyes turned a bright green and he turned back into the white cat.

Draco was ready and blundered out of the backdoor running towards the flower house. The hedge portal started to glow. Jinx's eyes were wild with excitement and Draco just trembled. "Jinx, I don't think I can go, I'm too scared." Draco hunkered down with his tail between his legs.

"Draco, we need you, you can do this," said Jinx.

By this time, the portal swirled with electricity and Jinx knew they only had a small amount of time before it closed, or they would miss their chance.

"You go first," Jinx said to Draco, "I can give you a nudge if I need to."

Draco lined up and jumped towards the hedges and into the portal he flew with Jinx close behind him. They twirled and twisted all through the hedge portal's tunnel and landed with a thud on the greenest grass Draco had ever seen. Jinx landed in the buttercup plant with flowers covering her face.

"Whew, we made it," Draco yapped.

Jinx brushed the flowers from over her eyes and hissed at the creature in front of her.

Draco said, "Hey Jinx what's wrong, it's just me, Draco."

Jinx stumbled upon the words to say, "Drrra dra Draco . . . You're a dragon."

Draco barked with surprise, but fire shot out of his mouth as they looked down the sapphire road to the hedge fairy realm.

Chapter 5

Draco's Dragon Journey

"The hedges are just in the distance," said Jinx.

Draco, still shocked by his new form, was staring at his outstretched wings in amazement. He barked and more fire rushed out of his mouth. He felt more powerful than ever. He started to walk but, just as Jinx sprinted ahead Draco stumbled and fell on the ground.

"Jinx," Draco cried, "I'm not sure I can

do this. I feel like I am going to hold you back."

Jinx turned and looked into the big dragon's eyes and said, "Draco I know you're in there! And I know you can do this. I can go slower until you get used to your new form."

She still saw Draco's heart in his big brown eyes, and they headed off towards the hedges together.

Meanwhile, Merkle, Merlina, and Rosy Q were on the other side of the hedges. They waited for the right moment and suddenly, the hedge portal started to spiral. Rosy and Merkle gave each other a big hug and just as Rosy started to enter the portal a white flash jumped past them into the portal.

"Kallan," scowled Merlina. "What will we do with him, Merkle?"

"There is no time to think of that right now," Merkle insisted. "Rosy do you have your book; I have a feeling you might need to use some of your crystal magic with Kallan."

"Don't hurt him," begged Merlina. "I know he can change, somehow."

Rosy Q looked into Merlina's eyes, "I don't know why you forgive him so much, but I will make sure he returns safely."

With that, she entered the portal and was gone.

Merlina and Merkle looked at each other and at the same time said in unison, "I hope she is ok."

They walked back towards the village to

make the final preparations for their guests of honor.

As the duo walked along the pathway, Draco started to get more coordinated within his new body and started to trot along comfortably. They stopped by a stream to get a drink of water and when the steam started to come out of Draco's ears, they laughed and rolled in the grass. Draco snorted and two puffs of smoke came out of his nostrils.

This adventure was the furthest Draco had ever been away from the house and he found lots of excitement along the way.

Just as they started upon their walk again, Jinx hissed, "Watch out!"

Draco looked ahead and saw a beautiful white cat approach them.

"Jinx," Draco whispered, "it's a cat?"

"What do you mean a cat?" questioned Jinx. "As far as I know I'm the only cat in this realm because Merkle said so."

As they continued along the path the white cat came up closer and closer behind them.

Finally, Jinx called out, "Hi, I'm Jinx, what can I do to help you."

Kallan froze and said, "I'm bringing blessings from Freda. She sent me to make sure that you two don't get into trouble."

Jinx answered, "I'm pretty sure that we are looking for Rosy Q but thank you for your help."

They continued but Jinx knew that the cat was still close behind. After all, they weren't too far away from the Wise Oak Tree, where they intended to meet Rosy Q.

Jinx held the obsidian talisman close to her and Draco clutched the healing quartz a little tighter. Something didn't feel right, but if they stopped to worry, it would only keep them from getting to Rosy Q quickly.

Eventually, they saw Rosy up ahead under the Wise Oak Tree. The air was heavy with tension as they approached. Even though the walk was only about an hour-long, in fairy time, to Jinx and Draco, it felt like days.

Human and fairy time are different.

Time passes much more slowly in the fairy realms. They had actually only been gone for only a few seconds in the human realm, but the time difference can leave you exhausted until you get accustomed to the change.

Finally, they were within a few feet of Rosy and the white cat suddenly darted in between the duo and Rosy.

"You will have to pass this test before you can enter my realm" growled Kallan.

"Don't do this, Kallan," warned Rosy.

"Or what, you'll come after me with your magic rocks?" he hissed.

Rosy opened her book and got out a powerful quartz crystal that was smoky in color. "This smoky quartz crystal will turn a negative into a positive Kallan. Now back away and let them pass," demanded Rosy.

Just then Kallan's eyes started to glow fluorescent green and the ground started to shake.

A huge crack in the earth began to open which revealed a huge ravine and an entrance to the cave fairy realm below. The ravine led down, down, down to a dark abysmal world of dragons and dark fairies.

Kallan looked back to Rosy and said, "Your sweet magic doesn't overpower me anymore."

He scratched her and she fell unconscious on the ground and Kallan quickly threw a large net over her before he vanished in a hazy smoke.

Jinx could see the smokey quartz as it lay on the ground and felt helpless to be able to assist Rosy.

Draco paced back and forth and whimpered in a worried frenzy.

"Hold yourself together," Jinx exclaimed. "We can do this."

Just as Jinx started to give up all hope, she remembered that Draco was no longer a dog. Draco had wings!!! He could fly!!!

After she estimated the distance in the crack, Jinx looked at Draco, who at this point was rocking back and forth like a coward.

"Snap out of it, Draco, you have wings, you can fly!!!" Jinx said with determination.

"I have never flown before Jinx, I don't even know how to use these things," Draco grumbled.

"Well, get up and let's practice," Jinx insisted.

Draco hesitated and then realized he had to at least try. He stretched his wings out and started to gallop and flapped and flapped but he landed flat on his snout.

"Awwwhhh," Draco cried.

"Try again," Jinx persisted.

He took another run and opened his wings and the air caught underneath and lifted him into the air. As soon as he started to flap, he tumbled down and rolled to a halt into a big boulder.

"Ohhh, this is hopeless," murmured Draco as he felt sweat dripping off his brow.

But Draco was determined and decided, he had to try one more time.

Jinx said, "Listen Draco, to do this you have to believe in yourself. Don't doubt yourself, even for a moment."

As Draco stood up, he closed his eyes

and felt the breeze across his rough skin. He felt the new sensation and concentrated on the breeze gently brushing his skin instead of his fur. He opens his wings and felt himself effortlessly lifting off of the ground. This time as he flapped his wings, he started to rise higher and had more control.

Jinx jumped on Draco's back and shouted, "Go Draco, over the ravine!"

Just as Draco moved forward towards the canyon he looked down and became frightened by the dark mist below. He started to plummet towards the ground and down into the ravine. They both cried out as they fell quickly but all of a sudden, they felt a strong power pull them upward.

Jinx looked up as Rosy Q yelled, "My smoky quartz always turns a negative into a positive."

They were gently placed on solid ground next to the Wise Oak Tree. Jinx gave Rosy a head nudge to thank her for her help.

But then with a shock, Jinx noticed Rosy had deep scratches in her cheek and Jinx looked at Draco saying, "Hurry, hurry, get the healing quartz.

Just as Draco reached for the gem, he realized that it had fallen out of his clutches when he was trying to fly. Draco had lost the healing crystal.

Rosy said, "There is no time to worry about that now. We must make it back to the safety of the hedge realm. Kallan might try something else."

Jinx held on tighter to the obsidian talisman in hopes that this magic would work against Kallan as they may need it to stun him.

They quietly walked the last few paces towards the hedge realm in silence.

Draco was devastated because he failed to keep the talisman.

Jinx was excited but worried about Rosy as she seemed weak.

Rosy Q bravely moved forward using her keen scent as she kept a close watch for Kallan. In the distance, they could see the hedge realm opening, but they also saw a white figure they thought must be Kallan as he waited there.

"Oh no," shivers Jinx, "There he is Rosy. What can we do?"

Rosy opened her Grimoire and said, "If my magic can't work on him then we have to make it work on us."

After looking through a few pages of crystals spells and enchantments, she sees an invisibility spell that her great grandmother gave her.

"This is an old spell that might work for us, an invisibility spell," Rosy reminisced.

She reached into her bag and pulled out the most beautiful fluorite crystal mixed with teal green and purple flashes.

"We can hold onto this as we slip past Kallan," Rosy said as she passed the fluorite crystals to Jinx and Draco. "The fluorite helps to balance and stabilize energies so it should keep us invisible long enough to pass Kallan."

As soon as she passed them out, she started with her enchantment.

Use the fluorite to protect and keep
We need invisibility, we need strength

"Now say it with me 3 times"

Use the fluorite to protect and keep
We need invisibility, we need strength

Use the fluorite to protect and keep
We need invisibility, we need strength

Use the fluorite to protect and keep
We need invisibility, we need strength

"Make it so."

All of a sudden, a glow came over and surrounded them in a hazy mystical cloud of purple and green. They were encased by the fluorite glow and they were inside of the crystal as they walked towards the hedge realm once again.

Now the hedge realm was within their reach. Jinx could smell the honey cakes and hear the fairies as they sang her favorite tune.

CHAPTER 6

THE HYDRA

The purple and green glow swirled around the trio as they made the last few steps toward the hedge fairy portal.

All of a sudden Rosy Q started to get dizzy and tripped as a puff of dust shot out from under her invisibility protection shield. Jinx and Draco gasped and helped Rosy to her feet.

"Go on without me," stammered Rosy Q. "You have to get to the protection of the Hedge realm."

Jinx looked panicked. "Not without you, Rosy. We will not leave you out here."

Kallan started to approach the injured hobgoblin with his eyes glowing. He prowled closer and closer knowing that Jinx and Draco were still there, but he couldn't see them because of the protection spell.

Rosy whispered, "You have to save yourself, I will be ok, just go bring Merkle back for help."

Kallan was getting closer and Draco was starting to breathe heavier. He was afraid he would breathe out a fire trail and ruin his and

Jinx's cover.

Kallan was closer than ever and all of a sudden Draco growled and fire came streaming out of his snout towards Kallan.

Kallan jumped back but as he looked towards Draco his face showed a fear like no other. Right behind Draco was a three-headed Hydra dragon aiming straight for Kallan. He cowed down and started to tremble. "Please don't hurt me," Kallan whimpered.

The hydra had been sleeping peacefully down in the cave realm below and when Kallan opened the ravine, it disturbed his hibernation.

"You have disturbed my slumber!!" the hydra said furiously. The Hydra continued, "You must pay, but if you will leave these travelers be, I will spare the worst and just provide this cage for you to be placed in so your magic will be turned to good. Just think of it as a rehabilitation crate."

Kallan said, "Please sir, I will do anything you want, just please don't hurt me."

Jinx and Draco were somewhat relieved,

but they knew that they hadn't completed the mission just yet.

Rosy Q coughed and she looked very pale. Her injuries must have been worse than they originally thought, and Jinx noticed a bruise on the back of her neck. She must have hit her head on a rock when she fell. She wasn't doing well.

Kallan was safely placed in the cage so all attention could be placed on Rosy Q.

The hydra then turned to Draco and said, "This quartz crystal talisman landed on my head during the whole ordeal back there. Does this mean anything to you?"

Draco looked in amazement and stuttered, "ye ye yes!!! YES. Jinx! It's the healing quartz talisman. Let's use it to help Rosy get better."

As they placed the talisman on Rosy Q's cheek a clear light came out of the crystal and filled her body with healing energy.

"Yes! It's working," Jinx and Draco celebrated together.

In the meantime, Kallan fumed angrily

in the cage. His eyes still glowed and were full of dark shadows. The hydra said, "I must return now to my cave with my family, please if you ever need my help again from this creature," he began as they all looked at Kallan … "Just say …

Hydra, Hyrda come to me
Hydra, Hydra help we need

Repeat it three times and I will hear your call for help."

They gave their goodbyes and gratitude as the Hydra turned to fly back to the cave.

Meanwhile Merkle and Merlina made their way back to the Hedge portal. "It has been way too long," worried Merlina.

"I'm sure they are fine," Merkle responded with concern in his voice. As they stood there waiting, Merlina was pacing back and forth with worry as the sun was already going down. The moon started to rise across the meadows with this silvery glow and they knew that the ceremonial hour quickly approached.

Just then the portal started to spin and with a huge sigh of relief Merlina and Merkle rushed over to the hedges. As they waited, they could hear struggles coming from the other side.

"Oh no," gasped Merlina, "that's Kallan's voice."

Merkle said, "There is nothing we can do right now because they have already activated the entrance to the realm. We just have to be patient and wait."

On the other side, Draco said, "Look ahead, the portal is already starting to spin for us."

The group hurried along, and they were closer than ever but, Kallan was rumpled in one side of the cage getting angrier, and started to shout for the trio to let him out as he clawed at the cage.

They continued to travel onward more quickly, and Jinx still clung to the obsidian stunning-spell crystal.

All of a sudden, Kallan started to grow. His fur fluffed out and his fangs grew larger. The glowing green eyes became fiercer and his claws grasped around the bars of the cage.

He got bigger and bigger and Draco said, "Oh no, he's turning into a tiger."

"A white one," said Rosy Q with concern in her voice. "White tigers are one of the most powerful magical beasts in all of the hedge fairy realm."

A loud ROOOAR came from him as he shook the bars with such force that he busted right out of the cage.

Jinx held up the obsidian and it stunned Kallan in midair.

"Wow, it worked," cried the trio at the same time.

Kallan came crashing down to the ground unconscious as they put him on top of Draco and pushed him through the Hedge Fairy realm portal.

Relieved, Rosy fell into Merkle's arms.

Merlina looked at her stepbrother in horror.

"I see you have met my stepbrother, Kallan. We must lock him in the dungeon now," she said sadly. "We can't let him ruin our night now. Welcome to the hedge fairy realm Draco, it is so nice to finally meet you both. Jinx, I understand that you have been here before, but we have never officially met."

"The pleasure is all mine, I assure you," said Jinx as she bowed to Merlina.

Merkle looked up at Draco and said, "You're a dragon now, that's delightful!"

Draco and Jinx followed the group to their preparation room so they could rest and drink some water. The hobgoblin guards hauled Kallan towards the dungeon.

"Kallan is taken care of for now," whispered Merkle.

"Tomorrow will be another story, we must figure out what to do with him, and fast," Merlina said to the new friends.

"I'm just glad we made it, and we always have the Hydra to help protect us if we need it," said Jinx.

"Now let's celebrate."

CHAPTER 7

*T*he silvery willow trees danced in the moonlight breeze with the smell of magic in the air. The hedge fairy realm was a magical place, especially at night. Draco chased the lighted critter bugs and Jinx admired the fluorescent fossil rocks. The Magnolia Tree sparkled with the purple and red flowers. It was truly a beautiful evening as the moon came up and gave a blessing for the special ceremony. They were tired from their journey, so they settled down to take a little nap before the festivities began.

The kitchen hedge fairies made the final preparations and the sarsaparilla was full to the brim even though Meryl had more than a few samples. The smell of honeysuckle vines drifted in the air, and the lightening bugs started to light up the night sky. As the stars twinkled, Jinx was roused from her nap and felt mesmerized by the bright colors and smells that filled the air.

"Draco, wake up, it's almost time for the ceremony," said Jinx with such excitement in her voice, a thrill she had never had before.

The magical atmosphere of the evening was contagious as Draco started to wag his dragon tail. His large tail swished back and forth knocking over the table. Jinx laughed at the clumsy creature.

"I have to get used to my size," he said with a chuckle.

Rosy Q came inside the room in a hurry to help them get ready for the feast and ceremony.

"You two are our guests of honor," said Rosy. "You need to look your best. Come with me for your baths and grooming."

Draco was excited because he loved getting baths, but Jinx; on the other hand, hesitated and didn't move.

"I'll just bathe and groom myself right here," Jinx insisted.

"No, you're coming with me," demanded Rosy, and even though Jinx arched her back to resist, off they went.

The baths were fancy with crystal counters and basins. Jinx was directed into the amethyst basin while Draco was led to a ruby and golden shower stall. Jinx had to admit, even if it was just to herself, that the water felt so refreshing over her fur. She relaxed into the massage of the fairies and looked over to see Draco looking upward into the water as it drifted downward out of the spout. He felt squeaky clean, which was a new sensation on his un-furry skin.

After a while, Rosy came back in abruptly and said, "Now it's time to get you ready.

My, don't you two look like a handsome duo, the other fairies are going to adore you."

As she looked at Draco she said, "The fairies will be excited to see we finally have a dragon on our side."

Draco bashfully said, "I will always do my very best to protect them, and you too, my new friend."

Merlina politely knocked on the jewelry maker's door, to get the special collars for Draco and Jinx. Rocky was the best jeweler of all in the Hedge Fairy realm and only the best was acceptable for Jinx and Draco. These collars would be presented as gifts of gratitude to the guests of honor. They also had been blessed by Freda with a special magic that Jinx and Draco would have to learn how to use. As she entered the room, she realized that the place was a mess and there lying on the floor was Rocky. Merlina checked for a pulse and could barely make out Rocky's heartbeat.

She called for Merkle. She and Rocky were secretly in love and they had not been able to announce their love yet because of the preparations for the ceremony. They had planned on doing it tonight during the feast.

Merkle came quickly with two nurses. "Take him to the infirmary, and quickly," Merkle said with a worried face. "Who could have done this," questioned Merkle.

After looking around the room for a moment they realized the collars had disappeared and they could see paw prints in the gold fairy dust on the floor.

"Kallan!" they both exclaimed at the same time.

They immediately rushed to the dungeon to make sure he was still secured. When they got there the two hobgoblin guards were tied up, with cloth in their mouths that prevented them from talking. Merlina ran over to find the dungeon door wide open and the chains broken.

"Thank you, thank you, Merkle and Merlina," said the guards as they were being untied.

"Kallan busted out of the cage and tied us up," they explained in a panic. "He said he was going to put an end to Draco and Jinx for once and for all."

Merkle looked at Merlina and then at the guards and whispered, "Oh no, Rosy Q is with them right now, we must get to them at once."

Rosy Q had watched and waited impatiently at the door for the surprise gifts.

"Oh, where could Merlina and Merkle be? They always waste so much time trying to get things done."

Rosy turned and looked at Jinx who had a purple cloak draped over her shoulders and back.

"Oh, our sweet Jinx, you look so lovely in purple."

She looked towards Draco who had a bright red cloak with golden trim.

"Oh, our dear handsome Draco, the color red suits you well. You could be Fairy Realm royalty," she crooned.

Just as she was about to turn to look for Merkle and Merlina once more, she heard a low growl in the crack through the door. This growl shook her to her core because she knew who it must be. Luckily, Jinx had brought the obsidian with her to the shower.

As Kallan busted through the entrance to the bathing area they all huddled together in terror.

"He has gotten MUCH BIGGER," cried Draco.

Kallan pointed his florescent green eyes directly at them. Jinx reached for the obsidian and held it tight. She knew she had two more times to use the talisman and she was prepared to use it. Just as he lunged forward, she held it up and he fell to the floor with a thud.

As Jinx looked over towards Rosy and Draco, she realized a bright aquamarine light coming forth from Rosy's hand and pointing towards Kallan's stunned body. This aquamarine crystal sent a shrinking spell to Kallan.

Just as Merlina and Merkle entered the room, Kallan went back to his fairy self. They cuffed his hands and checked his pockets. As they were moving him back to the dungeon, the two collars fell out to the ground and Rosy swiftly picked them up. The surprise gifts would have to wait until the ceremony.

At the infirmary, Rocky had not recovered from his injuries and Merlina paced back and forth in front of his hospital room. She saw him lying there lifeless. Jinx and Draco walked up behind her as she stared at the predicament.

"Merlina", said Jinx. "Yes," Merlina whimpered.

"We have the quartz healing crystal; would you like to use it.

"Oh yes," cried Merlina.

They walked over to the bed and placed the crystal on his forehead and the clear light poured out into his wounds just like with Rosy. Rocky started to gasp for air as Merlina put an oxygen mask on him. All of a sudden, his eyes opened and Merlina squealed with happiness to see her friend as he stared back into her eyes.

The nurse heard the commotion and ran into the room.

"Ok, ok," she scolded. "Let's give him his space to fully wake up and recover." She then turned to Jinx and said, "Thank you for your help. Now off you go.”

Just as Kallan went back into the dungeon, he started to wake up and realized he had been stripped of his power. The door slammed shut. Merkle and Rosy said to the guards, “Call us if you need any help.”

Rosy Q reached into her bag and took out her book. “Take this,” Rosy asserted. “This will cause his feet to turn to stone.”

“What crystal is this?” questioned the guards.

“This is the strongest crystal in all of the human realm, the black tourmaline which binds the poor unfortunate soul to the floor permanently” she cautioned as she looked towards Kallan.

Kallan shuddered in defeat.

“This is not the last you will see of me!” exclaimed Kallan.

“I will come after Jinx and Draco and defeat them.”

“Why do you have so much hate in your heart,” asked Merlina as she passed through the doorway. "This behavior is not acceptable. Here I was trying to give you a chance and all you do is try to cause so much pain and destruction. There are consequences for the actions you have taken part in and Freda will see to it that you are punished accordingly. Love and goodwill always prevail over hate and evil. Please try to be on the right side of this collaboration between the hedge fairies and humans."

Kallan scoffed, "Humpf, you think it's that easy to just forget how overlooked I was with father. Your mother just threw me away because I wasn't hers and they gave you the realm to lead and all I got was nothing but a measly head of security which now is taken from me because *'Draco will protect us all'*."

"We have to talk about this, but for now Freda and the ceremony await our arrival," said Merlina.

They hurried back to get Jinx and Draco ready for the big event.

CHAPTER 8

THE CEREMONY

$\mathcal{D}$ong, Dong, Dong.

The gong chimed three times as Merkle made his way from the Sacrosanct to The Magnolia Tree. A hobgoblin walked behind him with a hand drum providing the cadence for his journey to the ceremonial space.

Merlina fluttered behind him with a pillow and the crystal collars that Rocky had made. Merkle stood in the center of the circle and called for the ceremony to begin. All the

hedge fairies gathered around The Magnolia
Tree in great anticipation.

Merkle stood front and center and
proclaimed, "Cha ram lee ku ni, Cha ram lee
ku ni."

As the drumbeat quickened, all of
the hedge fairies started to chant along with
Merkle while holding their hands up high.
Hedge fairies are some of the most talented
singers and musicians in all of the fairy
realms. The sound of their collective voice
was majestic against the night air.

It was midnight and the moon shone
bright and full above the ceremony with
a silvery outline. The energy was high as
its power sparked in the air against the
moonlight.

All of a sudden, the chant intensified
and a beam from above brought forth Freda.
Jinx remembered what Freda looked like the
night she came to her. Her long white hair was
flowing, and her clear blue eyes intensified as
the chant came to a stop.

"Hear ye, hear ye," Merkle belted,

"Freda has joined us all for the initiation of Jinx and Draco into our Hedge Fairy realm. Our two worthy friends are here to provide a link to the human realm by delivering messages to and from the two lands. We hope the humans will heed our message and plant more green spaces for our fairy realms to enjoy. It is our esteemed honor to present for this important task, Jinx and Draco."

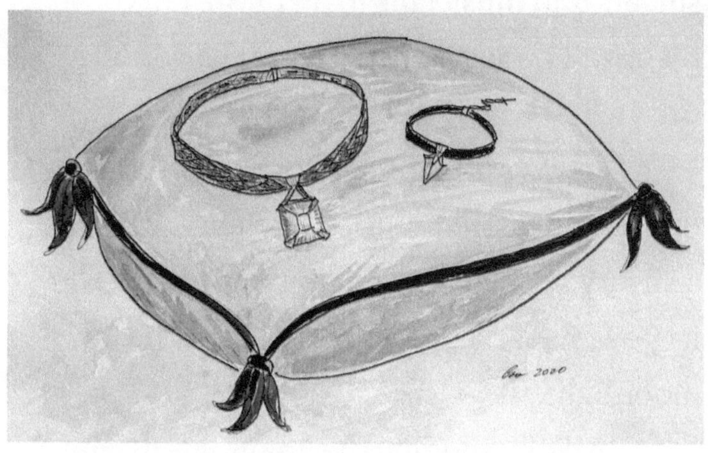

"Go, now!" Jinx whispered as she pushed Draco out from behind the curtain.

The pair joined the others, front and center, while the hedge fairies cheered. Freda, who had taken her place on the throne under the tree, rose and lifted her hand. All the fairies stopped and bowed their head.

She started to speak, "It is with great pleasure and heart that I hereby bestow the high honor of Honorary Hedge Fairy to Jinx of the Human World. This purple amethyst with a black velvet collar will guide Jinx and her intuition for communication between the human and Hedge Fairy lands." Freda turned to Jinx and said, "You will be a great guide for us to follow and bring peace and prosperity to both worlds. Please wear this collar with pride."

The hedge fairies cheered loudly and threw flower petals towards Jinx as she bowed to her new family and friends. Freda again raised her hand and all the hedge fairies stopped and bowed their heads again.

Freda then turned to the dragon, "Draco, you come with special protection skills and your assistance was necessary for getting Jinx here. Thank you for the love you have in your heart for Jinx. We also saw that love for a complete stranger, as you helped save Rosy Q in her ordeal with Kallan. Your strength, to guide us and the human realm together, is needed. It is with great pride that I present you with a Ruby and golden collar. The Ruby stands for the intense love you have for protecting those near and dear to you and the gold exemplifies power and royalty in our land."

The hedge fairies again cheered with glee but all of a sudden, the ground began to tremble, and darkness poured out from the dungeon across the village.

Merlina whispered, "Kallan . . ."

Freda then spoke, "One of your fairies has grown hardened by jealousy and rage, his heart has blackened. Please let us all take cover in the Sacrosanct. The darkness cannot overtake us in there."

As soon as the evening festivities moved indoors, it started to rain. A dark cloud came from the dungeon and brought an intense storm overhead.

The hobgoblin guards came into the Sacrosanct and exclaimed, "Kallan is using magic to do this."

Everyone gasped as Merkle assured everyone they were safe inside the Sacrosanct.

In the darkness and rain, the clouds covered the moonlight and Freda's glow began to weaken but Jinx had an idea.

Jinx rushed over to Rosy and asked for the selenite crystal. This crystal energizes all other crystals and acts like the full moon. Jinx gave Freda the selenite wand to hold and Freda started to glow just as vibrantly as before.

As Merkle sized up the situation with Kallan and with the guards, he realized that Kallan would only last a few more hours in the dungeon. His powers would eventually grow beyond silly weather change spells. They had to come up with a plan and—*fast*.

In an attempt to distract the fairies from the danger the fairy band started to play dance music. Jinx, Draco and all the other Hedge Fairies ate the delicious honey cakes and drank the sarsaparilla while some of the fairies danced. The fairy men clasped hands and circled around in pairs as the ladies danced in a larger circle on the outside. The men would trade-off into the direction of whichever fairy lady they wanted to dance with. In the end, the dancing stopped with the ladies and gentlemen split down the middle. Then the music started to speed up and the dancing became livelier. They clicked heels and grabbed hands as they spun around and around in pairs. The girl's dresses bounced and flowed outward while the boy's hats would nearly fall off.

While the fairies, Draco and Jinx danced, Merkle and Freda escaped to the meditation room with Merlina.

Jinx wondered, "What will happen to Kallan?" she asked while she looked at Draco.

"I have a feeling that he will be in a lot of trouble with ruining the full moon and our initiation ceremony," said Draco.

"I hope they don't hurt him; he just wants to feel like he belongs," says Jinx.

As Merkle and Freda discussed Kallan's fate, Merlina mentioned that she would like to see him change.

"Please don't hurt him," says Merlina as she started to cry. "I can't help but feel somewhat responsible for this. I stole all of the spotlight from Kallan when I was born. His mother died in a horrible accident and my mom never wanted anything to do with him. Our dad was too blinded by love to see what my mom was doing to Kallan. This throne should be his, but I don't see how his heart will rule justly."

After a few seconds she continued, "I could have been nicer to him too. All he wanted to do was have a companion and playmate when we all lived together."

Just as the party started to wind down, the fairies got ready to go home. They all saw the white cat, Kallan, pacing back and forth in front of the entrance of the Sacrosanct.

"Please everyone, we will all have to stay here tonight for our safety," said Merlina. "I will go and talk to Kallan."

As she approached him, it was still raining. He hissed at her.

"Kallan, I know you have it in you to be good. Please reconsider your actions before Merkle sends you to another fairy realm."

Kallan responded gruffly, "Oh, I have something much more interesting than Merkle's trivial magic spells. I will be king, Merlina, and I will rule here forever and ever."

Chapter 9
Oracles

*K*allan paced back and forth outside the Sacrosanct. He knew that as long as Freda was inside, his magic would be weak and the magic of Rosy Q and Freda combined could easily overpower him.

"Freda can't stay down here forever," Kallan taunted towards the fairies. "As soon as she leaves, I will take over and put this place into order again."

"Taken over by a stupid cat and mangey

mutt" complained Kallan as he mumbled to himself.

Inside the hut, all the fairies peacefully drifted to sleep and into a peaceful dream world. Merlina looked outside the Sacrosanct, she couldn't help but look out and feel bad for the angry creature. For one thing, as the rain poured down, she could tell Kallan was cold and most likely hungry too.

"Why doesn't he just let the love we all could give him inside his heart?" she questioned Merkle.

"His heart is hardened by years of jealousy," responded Merkle. "Any council I tried to give fell on deaf ears. He never admitted to any jealousy and lived in denial of ever being darkened by it."

Just then, Jinx's ears perked up and as she looked down, she saw her amethyst start to glow. Jinx closed her eyes to hear the voice that told her of events to come.

"Jinx," said the voice, "I am here to guide and warn you of events yet to come. My name is Amethia, I am an Oracle from the Crystal

Fairy Realm, and I speak to you through your psychic abilities that the amethyst amplifies." Jinx was dazed as Amethia spoke to her. She was a beautiful creature with lavender hair that flowed in the night breeze. Her face, with skin that glowed violet, showed peaceful serenity and her eyes, a deep purple, gave off a warm, loving energy. As the oracle turned her head, Jinx saw her ears were pointed and her lips were lilac and full.

"Only you can hear me, Jinx, the amethyst activates the part of your mind to hear from your future self. Here is your first prophecy foretelling hints of what's to come."

By the light of the moon
By the setting of sun
These fairies need your guidance as one.

The morn will come
And he will run
Use the dragon to get the job done.

Great, thought Jinx, but what in the

world does that all mean?

Amethia said, "Only you can decipher the riddle, use your love to guide you, and protect your newfound friends."

With that, the Oracle vanished into a purple mist.

"Jinx! Jinx! snap out of it," Draco insisted as he gently nudged her with his wing.

"What happened, what was I saying?" questioned Jinx.

"Something about an oracle and prophecy, I think you were dreaming."

Jinx looked into Draco's eyes, "No Draco, it's my amethyst, an Oracle speaks through it as a fairy from the Crystal Realm. Her name is Amethia and she gave me some instructions on dealing with Kallan. I think our mission is to now deal with him and save our new fairy friends."

Draco took a step back and wondered if he would have the coordination and control of his wings and body to be able to accomplish this mission.

"For now," continued Jinx, "you have

to get some sleep. Your ruby collar will guide you. I am going to meditate on this message." Draco turned and lay on his side while he closed his eyes. All he could do was toss and turn as he tried to go to sleep. He was so afraid he would fail his first mission.

Jinx went to the edge of the Sacrosanct and looked through the flower-shaped window where she saw Kallan hunched over asleep in the rainy night. She turned and observed the entire Hedge Fairy realm asleep peacefully around the sacred place. The sky cleared above the Sacrosanct and moonlight shone through the skylights in the roof, highlighting the beautiful arches inside the building.

Freda stood up and noticed Jinx deep in meditation at the flower window. Jinx slowly opened her eyes and adjusted her gaze to the pale moon light. She noticed Freda as she watched her admirably.

Freda walked over to Jinx and said in a soft voice, "This window was carved by my father the great Moon God, Filpe. He gifted this stone wall to the hedge fairies after the truce of the hedge fairy and flower fairy war. It is fitting that you meditate in this very spot as it symbolizes the union between two opposing forces. To bring Kallan over to your side will not be easy, but it can be done. Do not lose faith, my dear. I must return now that everyone is peaceful, and the rain is clearing." Jinx looked up with fear in her green eyes, but as soon as she looked towards Freda, she felt a peaceful warmth come over her.

"Thank you, Freda, thank you for this opportunity to find meaning in my life and also allowing me to bring my best friend Draco along with me. We will do the very best to bring union between Kallan and his family. We will not forget our larger mission to bring more green spaces for the fairies to live in." Jinx bowed her head and she felt Freda's presence rise into the clouds above.

Now they were on their own and they couldn't fail their first mission.

Jinx was awakened by the sounds of the

fairies singing their morning songs. It was the most beautiful music she had ever heard.

Bring us, goddess, a beautiful day
Bring us, goddess, a joyful day
Leave us with
Love in our heart

Bring us, goddess, a beautiful day.

After the last note finished, Jinx was startled by a growl behind her.

"I've always hated that stupid song!" grumbled Kallan.

Jinx backed up and looked into his eyes and said, "Kallan, let's make an appointment to sit together and talk in two hours. There has to be some way we can agree on the course of action."

Kallan lunged towards Jinx, but something pulled him back because Jinx was under the protection of the Sacrosanct. "I can't make any promises, but we can talk," snarled Kallan. He turned and strolled back towards his cottage with as much pride as he could muster. When he walked away, the fairies heard him as he mocked the morning song. Merlina came behind Jinx and said, "That used to be his favorite song when father was still alive. I do hope we can agree on a favorable outcome for everyone."

"Me too . . . me too," whispered Jinx.

Draco came over to Jinx with a shocked look on his face. "Jinx, the Oracle of Ruby, Ruther, came to me in my dreams," he said, his panting tongue hanging out. Ruther is the hydra from the Crystal Cave Realm. He rescued us the other day. He came to me with a prophecy, just like Amethia came to you," Draco excitedly continued. "Ruther said I am to protect and defend the fairies against Kallan."

Jinx thought for a second then said, "We will have to convince Kallan to back down. We are meeting with him here in the Sacrosanct in two hours to discuss the deal. I hope we do not fail but I feel these crystal collars have awakened super strengths in us that will help to guide us."

"Amethia said this:
By the light of the moon
By the setting of sun
These fairies need your guidance as one.

The morn will come
And he will run
Use the dragon to get the job done."

"Ruther told me the exact same thing," Draco said.

"I have an idea. Let's get him here and give him a deal. Tell him that if he will leave this realm, we will spare his life."

Jinx looked at Draco's big brown eyes, "What if he doesn't believe us? I think he wants more for himself than just to be in exile. We need to sweeten the deal."

At that moment Merlina, Merkle, and Rosy Q walked over to the table.

"Draco and I were just discussing Kallan's fate," said Jinx. "We both agree that he should be punished but not sentenced to death. We need to make him an offer to encourage him to leave this realm."

"He will never leave here," said Merlina. "He wants to be king. Maybe I should step down and give him the crown."

"NO!" everyone shouted at once.

"That can't be the answer," said Rosy with sadness in her voice.

"Yes, my dear Merlina, he will for sure put you in the dungeon forever," Merkle said empathetically.

The room became silent.

Jinx closed her eyes and started to say the message Amethia gave her in her vision. "he will run . . . dragon to get the job done . . ."

"That's it!" exclaimed Jinx.

Everyone was startled by her sudden outburst.

"We have to get him to run and Draco, you have to be the one to make that happen."

Chapter 10
The Battle

"We only have one hour to come up with a plan, Jinx," said Draco, looking a little anxious, his big eyes widening even bigger.

"I have no idea if I can even be successful at this. If Kallan turns into the white tiger again, I'm toast!"

Jinx looked at Draco and said, "Draco, you have to believe in yourself. We are all counting on you. We all believe in you. Let's see how you can use the Ruby for strength."

"I need some time to think, someplace quiet," Draco mumbled to himself as he walked away toward the back-meditation room of the Sacrosanct.

In the backroom, Draco looked around the private sacred space. He saw paintings and statues of Freda, and what seemed to be her parents and ancestors. The ceiling was made of golden panels that arched high above his head. The floor was a polished marble a golden outline around each carefully placed tile. The room was filled with energy which gave support for the mission at hand.

Draco closed his eyes and said out loud, "Freda, please guide me. Ruther, please give me strength." All of a sudden, he remembered the chant the Hydra had told him to say when he felt he needed help.

He started to chant quietly, "Hydra, Hydra come to me; Hydra, Hydra help we need." He said it again a little louder, "Hydra, Hydra come to me; Hydra, Hydra help we need." Nothing happened and Draco hung his head with a worried heart.

"I'll say it one more time," he said to himself thinking, "three times is always a charm. Then he chanted, "Hydra, Hydra come to me; Hydra, Hydra HELP WE NEED!!"

Just as Draco recited his chant the third time, the Ruby started to shake, and he looked down as the red began flashing brighter and dimmer, brighter and dimmer, brighter and dimmer … As he focused on the Ruby for guidance, his head started to grow larger and on either side of his head emerged two additional heads. His wings expanded and his body began to grow. He turned towards the mirror on the side of the room and was amazed at his reflection. He had transformed into an even more powerful dragon.

He was astonished at what he saw, Draco was a hydra!

As his heart raced, he rushed out of the mediation room.

Jinx's jaw dropped as she turned to see Draco. "You're a hydra Draco, how did you do that?" Jinx asked.

"I just asked Freda and Ruther for guidance and said the hydra chant three times, and this is what happened," said Draco.

The group went outside to the courtyard under The Magnolia Tree to wait for Kallan. As they waited, in the distance, just over the hedges, they saw the hydra as he flew just outside of the realm and hovered. Hydras couldn't pass into the Hedge Fairy realm, but they were able to meet at the edge and talk.

Draco walked over, and the hydra said, "I give you all my strength so you will know how to handle Kallan. You are a great warrior who will accomplish much with love in your heart. You already have love as your strength in your heart. The dragon head on your left will give you powerful strength to withstand

1000 armies. The dragon head on your right will give you quick wit and judgment to anticipate your enemies' every move."

With that, the hydra flew away into the distance. And with this explanation, Draco had developed more confidence in his upcoming battle strategy.

As Draco turned around, he told the fairies and Jinx, "We don't want to hurt Kallan, we just want him to understand that there is no place for his darkness here in the Hedge Fairy realm. His darkness will destroy this land and unless he finds a way to control it, he will have to leave. We have to banish him from the Hedge Fairy Realm until he finds his way into the light."

Merlina hung her head and as tears formed in her eyes she said, "I wish there was another way, but Draco, I am afraid you are right. Kallan's heart has hardened by Freda's request for change. If we do not follow Freda's advice, she will not keep her watchful eye over us and our hedges will continue to vanish. Bridging the human and fairy lands is crucial for all humans to understand that we need them to plant more gardens, flowers, hedges, and bushes for our realm to thrive. Kallan can't see past his selfish ways."

Just as Merlina finished with her speech, they all heard Kallan's voice from behind as he hissed his demands for a fight.

The white cat appeared and started to grow right before their eyes. "Draco, do you really think that your form is going to scare me, I can turn into the greatest magical creature of all the Hedge Fairy Realm."

As Kallan continued to grow larger and larger, he growled, and his fangs glistened in the sunlight. He lunged towards Merlina and Jinx, but Draco quickly put a fire protective ring around them.

The group all huddled together, and Jinx jumped through the fire as she surprised everyone including herself. Her body shifted and grew larger as she changed into a black panther. Her eyes glowed purple and her teeth sharpened while she growled towards Kallan. She started to pace back and forth in front of him.

Merlina pleaded, "Kallan, please back down, Draco and Jinx are too powerful with the blessings from Freda. You have no choice and I do not want to lose my only brother, my only family left to such darkness."

Kallan answered back in a low growl, "This is how you treat family? You have never accepted me for how I am so now you must face the consequences!"

With that, he roared and jumped towards Draco who pushed him backward into the hedge. Jinx leaped forward and trapped Kallan while Draco put his long dragon talon up near his throat.

"Kallan," said Draco, "if you cannot change you must run."

"Never!" insisted Kallan, "I will never be forced out of my home."
Jinx lunged forward landing on top of him while she held him down.

Kallan's powers started to fade. Kallan couldn't fight back. Just as Jinx looked away Kallan took his claw with his last bit of strength and stabbed Jinx in the chest as he pushed her off of him. She fell backward, with the wound bleeding all over the ground as Draco lunged towards Kallan and demanded him to run and never come back.

A portal started spinning and opening behind Kallan. Ruby Q stood behind them while she held the royal blue lapis stone high above her head. Draco pushed Kallan towards the portal.

Kallan screamed, "This is not over! I will find a way back! I will take back my realm if it is the last thing I do . . ." The portal swung closed with a great flash of light and Kallan was gone.

Everything fell into silence. All of the worry was suddenly focused on Jinx who lay on the ground, gasping for air.

Draco cried, "The healing quartz! Can someone get it? We have one more time we can use it before it has to be recharged."

Merkle ran over and pushed the quartz onto Jinx's wound.

Rosy Q headed over to lend a hand.

With a concerned voice, she said, "Guys this wound is deep, I hope this will work. Let's take her into the Sacrosanct."

Draco lifted her onto his back and placed her at the healing alter. As soon as he was inside, he shrunk back to his regular dragon size and bowed before her as he cried.

Merlina and Rocky washed her head with healing cedarwood oils. Merkle continued to hold the quartz over Jinx's wounds, and Draco continued to cry over Jinx, "Please Jinx, please don't leave me."

No sooner as the words came out of his mouth, a tear fell from his eye and into her wound. This tear of love caused the quartz to glow. A beam of light emerged from Jinx and she opened her eyes to take a big breath. Draco gasped, "Jinx, you're alive and safe!"

Everyone cheered!!

"You did it, Merkle, you did it!" shouted Draco.

"No Draco, your love for Jinx helped strengthen the spell, so your tear had the magic touch," said Rosy.

Jinx stood up and said, "No use crying now, we won!!!"

The fairies all cheered, and everyone hugged one another.

Merlina stood on the pedestal, cleared her throat, and pronounced for all to hear, "We owe a great debt of gratitude to Draco and Jinx. This new partnership will help us all thrive better than ever. Let us plan for a huge party and celebration later tonight."

Merlina looked over at Rosy and asked, "Where did you send Kallan?"

Rosy looked off into the distance and said, "Oh some place where he will find time to think. He went to the flower realm, which as you know is on the far side of our fairy universe. The only way back is to go through light so he will have to get rid of all that darkness before coming here again."

Jinx walked over and said, "Oh he'll be back, and we will be ready for him when he arrives. Right now, let's celebrate our victory."

Chapter 11

Celebration

"*H*ip Hip Hurray, Hip Hip Hurray!!!" all the fairies cheered with joy, as Draco and Jinx came into the circle around The Magnolia Tree.

Merlina stood in front of the fairies with tears in her eyes as she proclaimed that very day 'Draco and Jinx Day' in the land of the Hedge fairies.

They were the first 'outsiders' to ever have a day named after them, but they didn't feel like outsiders at all. They had found a second home with Merkle and the Hedge fairy realm.

"Today is a day we will always remember, where good won over evil, lightness over darkness, right over wrong. Kallan will always be a member of our realm but he will have to make the decision to come back with a softened heart."

Merlina paused, then said one last thing, "We will have a union between the human and fairy world and hopefully we can unite other realms of the Fairy lands with Draco and Jinx by our side."

All the fairies cheered with joy as the

music and dancing continued.

It was the last night of the full moon festivities and Jinx and Draco knew they had to get back home. Their human friends would be worried about them if they didn't return soon.

Jinx had tears in her eyes as she knew she would miss them all terribly.

"Merlina, thank you for this opportunity, this whole adventure has given my life such meaning, and I promise to support this union in any way I can."

Draco stepped up and gave Merlina a huge nudge, which almost knocked her over.

"I, my queen, will do whatever I can to help protect you all from any danger. Please know you can call on me at any time and I will help as I see fit. But for now, are there more honey cakes and sarsaparilla? I'm starving!"

Just as Draco and Jinx joined the singing and dancing a white beam of light shone down over the Sacrosanct.

"Freda!" exclaimed Merkle and Rosy Q all at once.

All the fairies made their way over to see Freda standing at the platform in the Sacrosanct. They bowed before her as she spoke.

"Fellow Hedge fairy citizens today is a great and new day for our realms. Jinx and Draco are our new leaders in this merger, and we should be ready for some amazing changes. Jinx, your vision for the future is strong, and Draco, you truly do have a heart of gold. You could have killed Kallan but instead you showed mercy. Both of you showed compassion and strength which is needed for the task at hand. Today is a great day for us all. Three cheers for Jinx and Draco,

"Hip hip ... Hurray!!" chanted the fairies. "Hip hip ... Hurray!!, hip hip ... Hurray!!"

As the fairies continued to clap and cheer, Jinx became aware she was getting a vision from the amethyst. The vision showed Jinx of many struggles yet to come, but the future was full of peaceful union between the human and fairy worlds.

"The future is indeed bright for our two lands," she said to Freda.

"Yes, there will be struggles, but seeing how you and Draco handled this first task, I know you will succeed in many more tasks," Freda complemented them with encouragement.

The stars shone brightly over the Hedge fairy realm and it was an extraordinary night with a magical feeling in the air. Jinx relaxed by The Magnolia Tree and enjoyed the last few hours before she and Draco had to make their way back home.

"Jinx," Draco said. "We are so lucky to have one another. Not many dogs and cats could be best friends like us."

Jinx looked over to Draco and nuzzled close taking a little nap before the journey home. In the background, they heard the beautiful songs of the fairies which helped them to drift off to dream world.

It was sad, this adventure was almost over. At the dawning hour, bright and early the next morning they would have to make their way through the portal and across the ravine that Kallan made. Then, they would continue on their way home through the hedge portal into their backyard.

That night Draco and Jinx both dreamed of all of the excitement and enchantments that the fairy realms brought them. Visions of future adventures bounced all around Jinx's mind as Draco dreamed of chasing dangerous creatures and flying as a hydra.

In her dreams, Jinx visited far off realms with flower fairies, mermaids, air sprites, and crystal caves. Draco dreamed of flying off in the distance as they both met indescribable creatures and extraordinary beings.

Before they knew it, Merkle and Rosy nudged them to wake up because the portal was about to open at the dawning hour.

With a sad heart, Jinx hugged Rosy Q and Merkle. "I am going to miss being here so much," she said to Merlina. "You have an amazing place here full of magical energy."

Draco looked at Freda, "Thank you,

Freda, for believing in me when I didn't think I could defeat Kallan. It really does mean a lot."

With a few more hugs and tears in everyone's eyes, they made their way to the portal in the hedges. As soon as they arrived there, the hedges started to spin.

Rosy Q said, "Oh, one more thing. Here, Jinx, this stone is a magical reflective crystal ball so you can call me anytime and talk. And Draco here is the dalmatian jasper crystal which will help dispel all negativity and keep you safe from harm."

As she held her hand up, she continued, "Now go my friends and return to the humans sharing this message with them. There is more than meets the eyes in our natural world. Open your eyes so you can see what nature has to offer if only you would plant a garden, flowers, or a hedge in your backyard."

With one last goodbye, Draco and Jinx were through the portal into the meadows on their walk towards home.

Chapter 12

Back Home

At last, Jinx and Draco could see their hedge in the distance. It felt like they had been gone from home for months, but it had only been a couple of days in the fairy realm. In the human realm, that was only twelve hours!

They were pretty much silent as they walked the journey back as both of them felt sad, they had to leave. Draco easily flew over the ravine which proved that he was now able to control his dragon self.

Jinx missed her human friends so much she was excited to cross the hedge portal into her backyard. Draco was ready for his human friends to pet him and feel the wind in his fur once again.

As they ventured closer towards the hedge it started to spin and they walked through to home. Inside, Draco turned back into a dog again and started to bark but this time without fire coming out. Jinx felt relief as she saw her sitting post on the fence there as it seemed to wait patiently to hear all about her adventures. Draco immediately went to the door to get inside the house, but Jinx hid. She wanted to sit and meditate on all of the adventures and to contemplate the future as a powerful figure in the hedge fairy realm.

Once the humans had taken Draco inside, Jinx went to the fence post to meditate. She was very happy and content. She looked around her backyard and home as she felt lucky to have such a loving family who helps take care of her. How would she ever deliver the message for the humans to plant more hedges? This task would be difficult but that was for her to figure out later.

"Ah" she sighed, "it's good to be home."

Just then one of her humans came to the door and called her name so she ran inside to get her snuggles and back rubs. As she was inside, she overheard the humans as they talked about planting a larger garden outside. She was pleased to know that even though it wasn't a hedge at least her humans were encouraged to plant more greenery in the backyard.

The little boys jumped around like monkeys and hugged them which showed how much they miss her when she sneaks out to the Hedge Fairy Realm. Although they are always full of energy, she knew they loved her and Draco with all of their might. She settled down on her spot on the windowsill for a much-needed nap after she ate some food and had her backrub.

Later that afternoon and into the evening she heard a commotion outside.

Draco, as usual, ran to the window and started to bark. This time he was barking, "Merkle, Merkle, and Freda too!!"

Of course, the humans just thought he was out of his mind barking at some bird, but Jinx knew she had to find a way to escape. She walked over by the door as Draco frantically tried to open the back door. The human finally lets him out and they both escaped. Jinx sprinted over to her post on the fence and settled in to see what Merkle might need. As she is on the fence post her amethyst starts to glow and she remained quite to receive the message.

It was Amethia, to reveal another prophecy.

Amethia approached her dressed in her purple and lavender flowing dress but this time with a silver trim.

"Hello Jinx, I foresee a "newcomer" who is all black and a cat. This black cat will be the chosen one who will guide all the fairy realms and human lands to unite for the first time ever."

With that message, the oracle started to fade away.

"Wait!" insisted Jinx. "Wait, what is this

newcomer's name? I have so many questions."

"As with all messages I cannot reveal any more. Love and blessings to you my dear Jinx." She disappeared into the misty evening air leaving Jinx with more questions than answers.

Who could it be? Jinx fits the description perfectly. "Could I be the 'chosen one'," she questioned out loud.

"The chosen what?" questioned Draco.

"Nothing. Never mind. I was just thinking out loud about something," Jinx persisted.

Draco shrugged and galloped his way inside.

Jinx sat alone on the fence post as she thought about what Amethia had said.

Then, all of a sudden, she heard Merkle just over the fence in his meditation spot.

"Cha um ray um zooooom, Cha um ray um zooooooom" Merkle chanted as Jinx watched curiously from the fence post. Merkle was in a full trance with golden pixie dust sprinkled all around. The grass glistened as he continued his chant. He called out to Freda who was also told of the prophecy of a newcomer who would help strengthen the connection between the human world and the fairy realms. Jinx again seemed to meet the description of this "chosen one" but she didn't want to let them know she knew just yet.

As she overheard this news, her excitement grew, and she had high hopes to become an even more important figure in the fairy realms.

All of a sudden, she heard a hustle and bustle in the house and Draco barked with authority, "Jinx, come here! There is a new kitten who looks just like you."

"A newcomer," thought Jinx "who looks just like me?" With a heavy heart, she slowly and begrudgingly made her way back to the house where she saw one lucky small tiny kitten.

"Meet Clover," said Draco with who overflowed with excitement.

She hissed with disgust and realized that maybe she wasn't the "newcomer" chosen one after all. She knew from the past few days she couldn't let jealousy overtake her heart. If there was one thing, she learned from Kallan, darkness will get you nowhere with the hedge fairies. But niceness would have to wait a day or so until she could form a plan to find out who was the real 'chosen one'.

After much thought, she understood that she had to follow her adventures to find the real truth. For now, the excitement of possibly being the chosen one would have to be kept a secret as she waited for her next chance to escape to the hedge fairies.

The back yard glistened as the rain drizzled down. The flowers, plants, herbs, and hedges breathed in the water as the leaves opened up to feel the water drip down.

All of a sudden, she heard the familiar sounds of the crickets and frogs as they sang the nighttime songs.

She sighed and thought about what Merlina was up to. Maybe she and Rocky finally got to announce their love for each other. Jinx hoped the rest of the fairies would accept their union. Rosy Q and Merkle, hopefully, were settled down with some romantic dinner and sarsaparilla of course.

She looked around her room and saw the humans as they watched the small humans run and play with Draco. She purred with the comfort as she sat in her own home. The new kitten, Clover, jumped and pounced at her tail as it swished back and forth, back and forth, back and forth. This annoyed Jinx, but she was too tired from her adventures to fight back.

The humans all got up and yawned as they made their way to bed. All was quiet as Draco laid on the couch next to Jinx and the new little one snuggled nice and sweetly next to him.

"Jinx," said Draco.

"Yes Draco," Jinx responded as she stretched her back and settled in for the night.

"I wonder what really happened to Kallan," Draco continued.

Jinx sighed and said, "I think he is somewhere learning his lesson. He sure will think twice before messing with my friend Draco."

Draco laughed and rolled onto his side.

He watched Clover stretch out, sit up and ask "What happened? What adventure? Who's Kallan? I want to go on an adventure.... Please!!!"

"No," said Jinx. "Our adventures are for

grown-ups for now you will have to wait and grow stronger."

Jinx secretly wanted to say that she was never welcome, but she knew that Freda and the oracle Amethia would know about her whether Jinx tried to keep it from them or not. She closed her eyes and tried to push away her jealousy.

She fell asleep on the windowsill dreaming of honey cakes, the beautiful Magnolia Tree, and her new friends. The memory of the sarsaparilla and the beautiful music danced inside her head. She couldn't wait to hear it all once again. She knew that she would be asked back soon. She needed to be asked back and quickly to find out if she was 'the chosen one.' She hoped it would be sooner rather than later.

Stay tuned for more stories of Jinx, Draco and now Clover. In the next book, Jinx will find out if she is the chosen one or will it be Clover?

The continued series will have the Trio going on adventures to different fairy realms. The flower fairies, water fairies, air fairies and much much more.

Visit our website at
www.JinxAndDraco.com